The WOMBLES

The Ghost of Wimbledon Common

Adapted by Elisabeth Beresford

from the Wombles television series produced by CINAR and UFTP

Hodder Children's Books

a division of Hodder Headline plc

It was early one morning and Orinoco, Bungo and Tomsk were all getting ready to tidy up Wimbledon Common.

"Off you go, young Wombles," said Great Uncle Bulgaria, "but wait a moment, where's Wellington?"

"Sorry," said Wellington, hurrying out of the Burrow and tripping over in his excitement, "but I've just finished my new invention! It's a kind of washing-up machine. There's just one problem - there's a lot of soap bubbles coming out of it!"

Not far away, a newcomer to the Common was busy working on her tree-house. She hadn't met the other Wombles yet, and Bungo and Tomsk didn't know there was someone living in the tree above where they were tidying. The wind blew through the tree branches and Tomsk and Bungo looked up, wondering how a lot of junk had got stuck up there.

Then, suddenly, they heard something rustling behind them. They looked round and there it was . . . coming straight towards them.

"It's a ghost!" said Bungo. "Quick, run, it's after us!"

They ran as fast as they could to Great Uncle Bulgaria.
"It was white as a sheet!" shouted Tomsk.
"It chased me," said Bungo.
"What's all this about?" asked Great Uncle Bulgaria.
"A ghost!" said Bungo and Tomsk.
"Nonsense," said Great Uncle Bulgaria,
going back to reading his newspaper.

Bungo and Tomsk decided they would catch the ghost
to make Great Uncle Bulgaria believe them.
They asked Wellington to help by
building a Ghost Catching Machine.

"I suppose I could use the parts
from the washing-up machine . . ."
"Just hurry," said Bungo.

Tomsk and Bungo went off with a butterfly net and a fishing
rod to hunt for the ghost. They didn't notice something white
floating in the air behind them. When Bungo and Tomsk
turned round and saw it they nearly jumped out of their fur.
And at that moment the ghost fell on top of them.

There was a wild scramble and then Bungo managed to
crawl out from underneath it.

"It isn't a ghost!" he said. "It's just an old sheet!"

Now while all this was
going on Wellington had
been making his Ghost
Catching Machine.
    "If any ghost comes
into our Burrow tonight
this will catch it!"
he said proudly.

That gave Bungo and Tomsk an idea. They put their heads together and decided to pretend to be ghosts that night.

So when everyone was asleep, they climbed out of bed and put their sheets over their heads.

"I'm a ghost," said Bungo, "whoooo!"

"I'm an even BIGGER ghost," said Tomsk, "WHOOOO!"

But no one woke up to see the ghosts.

So Bungo and Tomsk tiptoed through the Burrow until they reached the kitchen. And there on the table were some of Madame Cholet's special clover buns. They had to stop being ghosts for a moment just so they could eat one each. Delicious!

But at that moment Madame Cholet came into the kitchen.
"Ah ha!" she said, "two ghosts trying to steal my buns. Stop!"
And she chased the ghosts round the kitchen and then out into the hall. And as they ran round the corner, Bungo and Tomsk threw off their sheets. Tobermory heard the noise and came out of his workshop. He held up the sheets.

"There are your ghosts, Madame Cholet," said Tobermory.
"Wait a moment, what's that noise I can hear?"

The noise was a banging on the Burrow door - in the middle of
a storm with lots of thunder and flashes of lightning. Tobermory
threw open the door and they all looked out nervously. There -
right in front of them – was a ghost!

Everybody was very startled for a moment and then the ghost threw off its cloak.

"Hello! My name's Alderney and I've just come to live in the tree house. I hope you'll let me shelter from the storm. OH! That's my sheet you've got there. It blew away this morning!"

"I'm very sorry, your ghostliness!" said Bungo and everybody started to laugh.

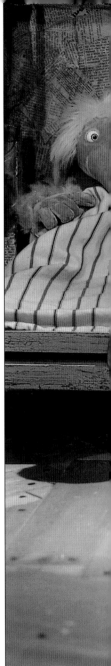

But that wasn't quite the end of the ghosts, because much later that night when everybody was tucked up in bed, Wellington's Ghost Catcher started to flash its light. Everybody woke up.

Bungo called out, "Madame Cholet, please come and turn off the machine! We don't want any more ghosts in our Burrow. Ever!"

Photographs and original artwork,
courtesy of FilmFair Ltd.
a subsidiary of CINAR Films Inc.

Copyright © 1997 Wombles Productions Inc.
(a subsidiary of CINAR Films Inc.) and HTV Ltd.
All rights reserved.
Text copyright © 1998 Elisabeth Beresford
based on the scripts from the TV series.

The Wombles ® is a trademark of Elisabeth Beresford/FilmFair Ltd

is a registered trademark of CINAR Films Inc.

ISBN 0 340 73579 1

10 9 8 7 6 5 4 3 2

A catalogue record for this book
is available from the British Library.
The right of Elisabeth Beresford to be identified as the
author of this work has been asserted by her.

All rights reserved.

Printed in Great Britain

Hodder Children's Books
a division of Hodder Headline plc
338 Euston Road, London NW1 3BH